UNLEASHED

Also by the John F. Kennedy
Center for the Performing Arts and the
White House Historical Association

Teddy Roosevelt and the Treasure of Ursa Major
Chasing George Washington

☆ ☆ ☆   ☆ ☆ ☆

UNLEASHED

☆ ☆ ☆ THE LIVES OF WHITE HOUSE PETS ☆ ☆ ☆

ADAPTED BY RONALD KIDD FROM THE PLAY BY ALLYSON CURRIN
COMMISSIONED BY THE JOHN F. KENNEDY CENTER FOR THE
PERFORMING ARTS AND THE WHITE HOUSE HISTORICAL
ASSOCIATION • ILLUSTRATED BY ARD HOYT

SIMON & SCHUSTER BOOKS FOR YOUNG READERS
NEW YORK LONDON TORONTO SYDNEY

SIMON & SCHUSTER BOOKS FOR YOUNG READERS
An imprint of Simon & Schuster Children's Publishing Division
1230 Avenue of the Americas, New York, New York 10020
This book is a work of fiction. Any references to historical events, real people, or real
locales are used fictitiously. Other names, characters, places, and incidents are products of
the author's imagination, and any resemblance to actual events
or locales or persons, living or dead, is entirely coincidental.
First Simon & Schuster Books for Young Readers paperback edition January 2011
Copyright © 2011 by the John F. Kennedy Center for the Performing Arts
All rights reserved, including the right of reproduction in whole or in part in any form.
Adapted by Ronald Kidd
SIMON & SCHUSTER BOOKS FOR YOUNG READERS is a trademark of Simon & Schuster, Inc.
For information about special discounts for bulk purchases, please contact Simon & Schuster
Special Sales at 1-866-506-1949 or business@simonandschuster.com.
The Simon & Schuster Speakers Bureau can bring authors to your live event. For more
information or to book an event, contact the Simon & Schuster Speakers Bureau
at 1-866-248-3049 or visit our website at www.simonspeakers.com.
Book design by Chloë Foglia
The text for this book is set in Bembo.
The illustrations for this book are rendered in watercolor with pen and ink.
Manufactured in the United States of America • 1210 OFF
2 4 6 8 10 9 7 5 3 1
Library of Congress Cataloging-in-Publication Data
Kidd, Ronald. • Unleashed / by Ronald Kidd ; illustrated by Ard Hoyt.—1st ed.
p. cm.—(The Kennedy Center presents Capital kids)
"Adapted from a play by Allyson Currin with the young
playwrights of Young Playwrights Theater."
"Commissioned by the Kennedy Center and the White House Historical Association."
Summary: The new president's daughter, and her pet chihuahua, take a tour of some of the
White House's previous first children and pets via a rattletrap jalopy time machine.
ISBN 978-1-4169-4862-9 (pbk.)
[1. Time travel—Fiction. 2. Presidents—Family—Fiction. 3. Pets—Fiction.
4. Chihuahua (Dog breed) —Fiction. 5. Dogs—Fiction.]
I. Currin, Allyson. II. Hoyt, Ard, ill. III. Title.
PZ7.K5315Un 2011
[Fic]—dc22
2010036594
ISBN 978-1-4424-1725-0 (eBook)

FIRST
F
EDITION

★ ★ ★ CONTENTS ★ ★ ★

CONTENTS

UNLEASHED

GO AHEAD, LAUGH

Arf.

Let me try that again.

Arf.

Look, I admit it's not much. But it's mine. My name is Tipp. I'm a dog, okay? Not a Doberman or a German Shepherd or a Great Dane. I'm a Chihuahua.

Go ahead, laugh. They all do. They think of a Chihuahua and picture my aunt Mildred, who rides around in a purse. Or my cousin Tiny, who wears a pink sweater and a baby bonnet. Poor guy.

If that's what you're thinking, forget it. I'm not like that. I'm different. At least that's what my owner tells me.

Her name is Alastair Lodge. She's beautiful. She's intelligent. She's gigantic. Hey, when you weigh three pounds just about everything looks big!

Alastair gives me dog bones and doggie treats. When I'm scared, she hugs me. When I talk, she listens.

That's right, I talk. Dogs talk. Get used to it. Kids have known it for years. It's grown-ups who don't listen. You know who you are.

Alastair listens, and I talk. A lot. Here's the thing: I'm just the tiniest bit nervous. My stomach bothers me. I have a problem with reflux. Mysterious rashes break out all over my body. Alastair tells me not to worry, which is like telling a hyena not to laugh. I cower. I quiver. I shake. It's just me, okay? It's what I do.

I was feeling nervous that day when Alastair and I arrived at the White House. Huh? Oh, I forgot. In all the talk about me, I didn't mention one small detail. Alastair's father, Aubrey Lodge, was just elected president of the United States.

Anyway, Alastair walked inside that first day, carrying her suitcase and a history book. I stayed outside on the porch. The porch was big and white—after all, it was the White House—and the lawn, surrounded by trees and bushes, stretched off into the distance.

"So, this is it," I heard Alastair say from inside. "Will you look at this place? It's huge . . . and beautiful . . . and ours! I'm the First Daughter. Do you believe it? It actually happened, just like Dad said it would. This is our moment in history, Tipp. Tipp? Where are you? Tipp!"

She spotted me on the porch. That's right, I was quivering.

"Come on, boy," she said. "You've got to look at this place. Every president since John Adams has lived here—and now us!"

"Do we get Secret Service protection?" I asked.

"Honestly, Tipp. You've got to see this. Come!"

Alastair and I took a dog obedience course a few years back. They taught her some commands. Sit! Heel! Come! If you ask me, it was a waste of time. But I obeyed because I didn't want Alastair to feel bad.

Gathering up my courage, I looked through the door, then crept inside. The place was just like Alastair had said. It was huge. It was beautiful. But she was wrong about one thing. It wasn't ours and it never would be.

Alastair grinned when she saw me. "Just think, Tipp, I'm the First Daughter! You know, that's quite an honor."

Setting down her suitcase, she opened her history book. "Look at this. It says that President Teddy Roosevelt's daughter Alice even had a *color* named after her: Alice Blue! What do you think my color would be? Alastair Orange? Lilac de Lodge?"

I tried to answer, but it came out more like a squeak.

Alastair closed the book and knelt down beside me. "Come on, Tipp. It won't be that different from the Governor's Mansion. We'll still have Mom and Dad and each other."

"Aren't you nervous?" I asked.

"Not at all! The White House is so cool. I've been reading about it. There's a pool and a pastry kitchen and a bomb shelter with gas masks . . ."

"Gas masks!"

She giggled. "You might as well learn to have fun with this. It's official: We've been elected!"

"No," I said, "your Dad was elected. Nobody asked me if he could run for president. *I* won't be able to take the pressure of the spotlight. I can't help it—it's my fine breeding."

"You came from the pound, Tipp."

"We'll be under a microscope. They'll be watching every move we make. What if they find out about"—I checked to see if anyone was listening—"you know, my seamy side. The untold story."

"Stop it," said Alastair.

"You know what I mean. The time I chewed through that extension cord? Bit that campaign manager? Peed on the carpet?"

"Relax," she told me. "No one's going to be talking about the presidential dog. It's always about the presidential *kid*!"

"That's not true," I said. "The American people *love* White House pets! They're obsessed with them. I won't have a minute to myself!"

"Oh, for Pete's sake, Tipp. I love you. You're my best friend in the world. But you've got to pull yourself together."

"I think I'm going to throw up," I said.

I MAY HAVE WHIMPERED

He wore a coat and tie. He carried a clipboard. And I could tell right away that he had never *really* listened to anybody, let alone to a dog.

He stormed into the room, talking on his cell phone. When he saw Alastair, he put the phone away. "Miss Lodge, I've been looking all over for you. You've got to get dressed for pictures."

"I'm sorry," said Alastair, "but who are you again?"

He beamed proudly. "Milo Connors, Official Protocol Adjunct to the White House Press Office, East Wing."

She looked him over. "You're pretty young for that, aren't you?"

He sighed. "Okay, *Junior* Official Protocol Adjunct to the White House Press Office, East Wing."

"Do you even shave?" asked Alastair.

He turned bright red. "I'm an intern, all right? But I'm working my way up!"

Hurrying over to a table, he set down his clipboard and pulled out a list. It spooled to the floor like a roll of toilet paper. "Okay, so today we've got the official White House publicity shots. Then there's a press conference in the Rose Garden—you don't have to talk, they just want you in the background. Then you'll do a meet-and-greet with the Girl Scouts. Didn't you get the memo?"

Alastair looked overwhelmed. "Wait a minute. Can't I unpack first?"

"We've got people to do that for you," said Milo. "Come on, America is dying to see you. Your father let you keep a low profile during the campaign, but now that we've won—yay!—the country wants a good look at you. You know, to sink their teeth into you."

I may have whimpered.

Alastair leaned over to me and murmured, "He doesn't mean that literally, Tipp. At least, I don't think he does."

Milo began pacing nervously back and forth. It seemed like a good idea, so I decided to pace right along with him. When Milo noticed, he jumped back and stared at me. "What is that thing? A rabbit?"

Alastair defended me, of course. "He's a Chihuahua, and his name is Tipp. He's my best friend in the whole world."

She scooped me up and held me close. Milo rolled his eyes. I would have thumbed my nose at him, but dogs don't have thumbs.

Milo started pacing again. "Now, where were we? Oh, right. You'll need to put on a dress. We're running on a timetable."

"You know," said Alastair, "I was really hoping to get a minute or two to look at my room. Do you think I could have the Lincoln Bedroom? My book says that in President Lincoln's day it wasn't a bedroom, but his office. Did you know that?"

Milo stopped and stared at her. "You think we have time for a history lesson? I could lose my job! Is that what you want?"

"No, but—"

"Do you know the kind of pressure I'm under?"

Alastair shrugged. "I thought you said you were just an intern."

"The press is watching every move we make, and they're hostile! Your dad hasn't even been in office a week and they hate me! Everybody here *hates* me!"

"Wow, I'm sorry," said Alastair. "But I don't see what that has to do with me."

Milo sighed and shook his head. He looked at Alastair the way she had looked at me the first time I pooped on the rug.

"Look, Miss Lodge. You're a kid. A kid with a pet. Everybody loves a kid with a pet. If people are making a big fuss over you, then they'll back off *me!*"

Alastair said, "You seem a little tense."

"*Tense!* I'll show you tense! Now brush your hair, put a bow on the rabbit, and *smile!*"

"He's not a rabbit!" she exclaimed. "He's a Chihuahua."

Suddenly I couldn't take it anymore. Hopping out of Alastair's arms, I raced over to the table and began clawing it. It's a nervous habit, okay?

"No, Tipp!" said Alastair. "Bad Tipp!"

She picked me up again. My paws were still twitching.

Milo rolled his eyes. "Can't you control that rabbit?"

"Chihuahua!"

Milo cleared his throat and got a funny look on his face. "Yeah, about that . . . uh, Chihuahua."

"What about him?" asked Alastair.

"I mean, sure, he helped win the California vote. But now that you're in office, the image consultants want you to get a dog who's a little more . . ."

"What?"

"Well," said Milo, "a dog who projects more confidence and power."

"Another dog?"

"You know," he said. "A replacement."

A replacement! For me? My pea-sized heart started pounding.

Alastair gaped at him. "You want me to get a new dog?"

"Hey, it wasn't my idea," said Milo. "It came straight from our focus group. How about a Lab? That's an all-American preppy classic. Or a German Shepherd? That says, 'America's in control!' Or a Collie? How about a Collie? The whole Lassie angle . . ."

Lassie! The old TV actress? What a phony she was!

Besides, I hear she looked terrible without her makeup.

Alastair said, "But Tipp is mine. I love him."

"You want some time to think about it?" asked Milo.

"No!"

"Take a week to mull it over," he suggested. "In the meantime, let's get this photo shoot over with. Happy all-American family, blah-blah-blah. You know the drill."

Alastair said, "But . . . can't I talk to my dad about this?"

"Hey, you're in the White House," said Milo. "You belong to the American people now."

He glanced at his watch. "Oops, gotta go. Don't forget the photo shoot. And please, put a ribbon on the rabbit." He bustled out of the room.

"Chihuahua!" she yelled after him.

When we were alone again, I shook my head sadly. "I'm sorry. I wish I was more like Fala."

"Who's Fala?" she asked.

I looked up at her, surprised. "You don't know? Fala, who was Franklin Roosevelt's dog? Fala, who had movies made about him? Fala, who had his paw on the pulse of the American dream?"

"He sounds impressive," said Alastair.

"He was the greatest dog in White House history," I told her. "I had a dream that maybe I could model my career after him. But who am I kidding? I'm nothing like Fala. I'll be a joke, a laughingstock."

"Don't say that!"

I sighed. "Do you really think they'll make you get rid of me?"

"No! Mom and Dad would never do that to us."

"But Alastair, we're not just a girl and her dog anymore. We're in the White House."

She held me close. "I won't let anyone take you away from me."

"But what if they make you?" I asked. "What if you don't have a choice?"

My stomach hurt. My paws ached. As we spoke, I could feel a rash breaking out. If this was life in the White House, I had just one thing to say:

I want to go back home!

A MASSIVE KEY RING

"How about a lemon drop?"

I didn't see him walk in. I didn't hear him. I didn't even smell him, and I'm pretty good at smelling. But suddenly, there he was.

I jumped out of Alastair's arms and scurried over to check him out. He was an older man, with dark skin and kind eyes. He wore a tuxedo, and his shoes were so shiny I could see my reflection.

"Excuse me?" said Alastair. "Have we met?"

Her voice shook, and I could tell she was a little nervous. Who was this guy? If he was anything like Milo, maybe we should just turn around and leave.

The man pulled a package from his pocket and held

it out to her. "Have a lemon drop. Have two."

I watched Alastair to see how she would react. She studied the man, and suddenly her face lit up. I love it when that happens.

"Oh, I remember you," she said. "My mom introduced us. You're Max, right?"

"That I am."

Alastair shrugged. "I guess I'll have one. Thanks." She took a lemon drop and sucked on it while thoughtfully gazing at Max. I could tell she was sizing him up.

He smiled. "I noticed Milo was in here. Don't let him scare you. Remember, it's his first week on the job too. He'll learn his way and calm down. They always do."

"Do you work for Milo?" said Alastair.

"Oh, no. I'm the Usher, but not like in a movie theater. I'm Chief Usher of the White House."

"What's that?" she asked.

"I report to the President and the First Lady. I'm in charge of the building, the food, the maintenance, and the household budget. And the housekeepers, the florists, the electricians, the cooks . . ."

"You must be very important," said Alastair.

"Oh, I don't know about that. Another lemon drop? Here, have the whole box."

Alastair hesitated, then took the box. "Well, these are awesome lemon drops."

"Special White House recipe," said Max. "You need top secret clearance to get them."

A special recipe? I wondered if they had a special recipe for kibble. Or for my personal favorite, steak tartar.

Alastair reached into the box and took another lemon drop. As she sucked on it, her shoulders drooped. "Just a few minutes ago I was so excited to be here, and then . . ."

Max watched her with those kind eyes. "I've been Chief Usher here a long time. I've seen a lot of First Families come through these doors. It can be scary at first, when you're a neophyte."

"Neophyte?" said Alastair. "Do they make a cream for that?"

Max chuckled. "No, no. It's just a word that means you're new at this."

Alastair flopped down into a chair, and I hopped onto her lap. She told Max, "But I'm used to politics.

I did fine when Dad was governor. It's just . . . nobody ever told me I'd have to give up my dog. Ever."

"Maybe it won't come to that," said Max.

"But what if it does?" she asked. "This may sound terrible, but for the first time, I don't want to be here. Not if it means giving up my best friend."

She gave me a hug. It was almost enough to make me forget what Milo had said. Almost.

Max gazed at me, then looked up at Alastair. "What if I said I could help you with that?"

"Huh?"

He pulled out a massive key ring. "You ever stop to consider keys? Think about it. The fewer keys you carry, the more important you are."

"I don't get it," she said.

"Does the Queen of England carry a house key? No, because she's important. Does the Prime Minister of India carry keys? No, because someone's always there to open doors for him. Now, look at how many keys I have. What conclusion does that lead you to?"

Alastair hesitated. "That you're . . ."

"Go on."

"That you're not very important?"

"Exactly!" said Max. "All I do is run this building. It doesn't sound all that important in the big scheme of things, not when you compare my job with what your father will be doing. But here's the catch: I've got keys to things other people don't even know exist. I've got all kinds of keys."

"Do you have a key to the movie theater?" asked Alastair.

"This one right here."

"The pastry kitchen?" she asked.

He nodded. "A couple of those."

"The bomb shelter?"

"How did you hear about that?" asked Max.

She showed him her history book. "I read about it in here."

Max glanced at the book. "I'll give you a tour after lunch."

"What are these other keys?" she asked.

Max pulled them up, one at a time. "This one opens the freezer where all the ice cream is kept. Here's the key to the game room. Here's the key to the chocolate shop."

Alastair grinned. "The chocolate shop? Cool!"

Just then, she noticed a big, old-fashioned key made of brass. Reaching out, she touched it. I could swear that it glowed.

"What about this key?" she asked. "What does it open?"

"Ah," said Max, "I was hoping you'd pick that one. This, my friends, is the most important key of all. It's the key to your problem."

SMELL DANGER!

The key to my problem? Had someone found a cure for eye boogers?

Max took the key off the ring and polished it on his sleeve. "This key can help you, but there's a catch. Can you keep a secret?"

"Sure!" said Alastair.

He said, "The White House has been around a long time. I've been around a long time. And between the two of us, we've tucked away quite a few secrets. Come on, I want to show you something."

Max turned to leave. Alastair said, "Wait! Can I bring my dog?"

"You mean, Tipp?" said Max. "Sure, but only if he'll be polite and say something."

Alastair glanced nervously at me. "Uh . . . but dogs don't talk."

Max chuckled. "You think I've never met a talking animal?"

"It's just . . . well, I've never known a grown-up who . . ."

"I'm not just any grown-up," said Max. He bent over and held out his hand to me. "Hello, Tipp. How are you today?"

I didn't know what to do. I didn't usually talk to grown-ups. Alastair knelt down beside me. "It's okay, Tipp. I think we can trust Max."

I shrugged. Dogs can shrug too, you know. I said, "My nerves are shot, but otherwise I'm fine."

"Glad to hear it," said Max.

Alastair clipped a leash to my collar and picked up her book. We followed Max to a corner of the room, where he approached a big painting of George Washington. Reaching out, he swung open the painting, revealing a doorway. He walked through and motioned for us to follow.

I liked it. A doggie door in the White House!

We found ourselves in a new room, where there was something that looked like an old, rickety jalopy.

"Nice!" I said. "What is it?"

Max answered, "That, my new friends, is your escape route."

Alastair stared at him. "Say what?"

"Your escape route," said Max. "This car will take you back in time to a place when you and Tipp were safe together. You can stay there until all this nonsense blows over. A new dog? What a ridiculous idea!"

I turned to Alastair. "Hey, I like this guy!"

"It's a time machine?" she asked Max. "For real?"

"For real," he said. "Do you have a place in mind? A time when everything was safe, and you and Tipp were happy?"

"Of course!" she said. "The old clubhouse I had when I was eight."

Max nodded. "Then that's where you're going. Or rather, that's *when* you're going."

He opened the door to the jalopy, put the old brass key into the ignition, and helped Alastair inside. Sitting

down, she set the book in her lap, blew dust off the steering wheel, and gave my leash a little tug. "Come on, Tipp. Get in."

Suddenly, alarm bells went off. Not real ones, but the kind you hear in your head when something is wrong.

I yipped, "Smell danger! Smell danger!"

"Tipp, cut it out!" said Alastair, but I could tell I'd planted a seed of doubt. I wasn't the only one who was nervous. She turned to Max, and her voice quivered. "Time travel isn't dangerous, is it?"

"No more than a walk on the National Mall," he said. "Just one thing, though. Don't touch the red button."

I looked inside and checked the dashboard. Sure enough, there was a big button in the middle.

"Why shouldn't we touch it?" asked Alastair.

Max scratched his chin. "Well, now, no one knows exactly. The one person known to have survived the red button came back muttering only five words: 'Don't talk to the snake.' That was it. 'Don't talk to the snake.'"

"What does it mean?" she asked.

"I don't know," said Max.

"Well," said Alastair, "you don't have to worry about me touching any red button. I'm deathly afraid of snakes."

She tugged my leash again. "Be brave, Tipp. We can do this."

My alarm bells were still clanging. "No," I said, "don't make me!"

"Come on, Tipp," she begged. "For me?"

I sighed. How could I resist? My master, leader, and best friend said we should do it. Who was I to say no?

I stepped inside, and the jalopy roared to life. The floor started shaking—or maybe it was me.

"Does this thing come with a barf bag?" I wailed.

Before anyone could answer, a strange voice boomed out. "Official greetings!"

I'm not saying I was surprised, but if you check the *Guinness World Records*, you'll find my name under "Highest Vertical Leap by a Chihuahua."

Of course, I soon figured out where the voice was coming from. It was the car!

"Thank you for being with us today," said the voice. "Sit back, enjoy the ride, and keep your hands and feet in the jalopy at all times."

"How about paws?" I asked.

"Those too," said the voice.

Alastair turned to Max, who watched from outside the jalopy. "Any last-minute instructions?" she asked.

He smiled. "Just enjoy your trip!"

Alastair picked me up and put me in her lap. Then, taking a deep breath, she commanded, "To my clubhouse!"

The jalopy sputtered, then rose into the air.

OOPS

"OMG, this is so cool!" exclaimed Alastair. "Look how high we are!"

I would have looked, but that's hard to do when you're hiding under the seat.

The voice of the jalopy boomed out again. "If you look to the right, you can see the Washington Monument and the Tidal Basin. Keep your eyes wide open as we pass over the Jefferson Memorial and the north bank of the Potomac River."

Alastair pointed and called excitedly, "Look how itty-bitty the paddle boats are! Like ants!"

"This is a terrible idea," I said. "Get me home!"

Jumping up on the seat, I started pushing buttons

frantically. Alastair tried to stop me. "Tipp, wait! What are you doing?"

Wasn't it obvious? I was panicking! It's what I do best.

I shrieked, "Must! Get! Down!"

As I punched more buttons, the jalopy's voice faltered and started to break up. "Keep your eyes peeled for . . . on the Capitol Dome . . . best view of Pentagon . . . dooo-werp-booooo . . . mooooooooooooo . . ."

Alastair shouted, "Not the red button, Tipp! Not the red button!"

Oops.

The jalopy made a sharp turn to the left and banked through the clouds. Lights flashed. Horns sounded. We were heading straight for the ground! Alastair grabbed me. We closed our eyes and held on tight, waiting for the crash.

There was no crash.

We opened our eyes. The jalopy had landed. But where were we? There were trees and grass. There were bushes and blue sky. There were birds.

"Okay," said Alastair, "this is *not* my clubhouse!"

Someone was whimpering. I think it was me.

"What did I do wrong?" I wailed.

Alastair said, "Did you hear what Max told us? Don't push the red button!"

"Hey, I'm a dog," I said. "I'm color blind."

She set me down, dusted herself off, and climbed

out of the jalopy. Spotting a crank on the front, she leaned over and turned it. The engine wheezed but didn't start. She tried again and again, but it was no use.

"Well, this is just great," she said.

I huddled in the front seat. "You think the jalopy's broken?"

"How would I know?!"

"Don't yell at me!"

Alastair took a deep breath. "Okay, okay. Let's stay calm here. Max knows where we are. If we don't come back, he'll send someone to find us."

"What will we eat until then? Remember, I get low blood sugar."

"I'll figure something out," she said.

I studied her face. "Are you mad at me?"

Her expression softened. "Oh, Tipp. You're too cute to be mad at."

"Cuter when I wag my tail."

I gave her a demonstration. Smiling, she walked back around the side of the car, picked me up, and gave me a hug.

"Don't worry," she said. "The Chief Usher of the White House would never send us someplace dangerous. Once the jalopy cools down or whatever, it'll deliver us to my clubhouse, safe and sound."

She noticed her history book on the floor of the jalopy. Picking it up, she read something on one of the pages. "'The only thing we have to fear is fear itself.' Hey, I've heard that before. Franklin D. Roosevelt said it."

There was a loud noise, halfway between a bellow and a roar.

"Okay," I said, "now we have something else to fear."

As I quivered uncontrollably, the bushes parted and two goats came bursting through. They were pulling a chair tied to them with ropes, and in the chair was a boy dressed in old-fashioned clothes. He skidded to a stop right in front of us.

"What a ride!" he said. When he saw us, he blinked in surprise. "Who are you?"

"Who are *you*?" asked Alastair.

"I'm the First Child," he said.

"*I'm* the First Child," said Alastair.

"My father's president," he said.

"*My* father's president," said Alastair.

I looked around. "Is there an echo in here?"

The goats stared at me. "Well, what do you know," snorted one of them. "A talking rat!"

"Chihuahua!" I said.

"Now, that's just weird," muttered the other one.

"No weirder than talking goats," I snapped. I didn't want to say anything, but they did more than just talk. They smelled, big time. Can you say BO?

Meanwhile the boy climbed to his feet, staring at the jalopy. "What is that thing?"

"Don't ask," said Alastair.

He ran his hand over the fender, then approached Alastair. "I'm Tad Lincoln," he told her. "These are my goats—Nanny and Nanko."

"I'm Alastair Lodge. My dog is Tipp. And I hope you've got better manners than those goats."

"I sure do," said Tad, shaking her hand. "Welcome to the White House!"

Alastair looked around. "The White House! Is that where we landed?"

"Well, it's the backyard," he said.

She shook her head sadly. "And here I thought we were going back home to my clubhouse."

"Not this year, you're not!" said Tad.

"What year is it exactly?" she asked.

"What kind of question is that?" he said. "It's 1862, of course!"

Alastair looked at me. "Uh-oh, Tipp, we're in trouble. This thing sent us back in time all right—to the wrong time!"

GOAT COMEDIANS

Alastair looked at Tad. "I guess that means you're . . ."

"That's right," said Tad. "I'm Abraham Lincoln's son."

Okay, I'll admit I was impressed, even if his goats did smell. But I was more worried about our ride home. I said, "I don't suppose you have any idea how to run this jalopy, do you?"

"No idea," Tad answered. "Nanny, what about you?"

"I don't know how to run it," said the smaller goat, "but that fender sure looks tasty."

"Aw, she's just kiddin'," Nanko said, laughing. "Get it? *Kid*ding? Kid? Like a baby goat?"

"Good one!" bellowed Nanny. The two goats clicked hooves.

Great. We'd traveled a hundred and fifty years to find a couple of goat comedians.

Tad faced us with his hands on his hips. "So, you're the latest team in the White House. They should have told us you were coming."

Nanny looked us over. "You call this a team? A girl and a rat?"

"Chihuahua!" I said. "I'm a dog."

She grinned. "Really? Hey, doggie, stand up."

"He *is* standing," said Nanko.

Nanny grinned. "Whoa, another good one!" They clicked hooves again.

"Your goats aren't very nice," said Alastair. I love it when she stands up for me.

"Well," said Tad, "you have to admit, your dog is kind of small. I'll bet he doesn't eat much at all. Not like Nanny and Nanko here; they'll gobble up anything. You should have seen my pa when they ate the first draft of the Gettysburg Address!"

Alastair said, "Just go easy on the teasing. Tipp's a little sensitive."

"He's a scaredy cat?" said Tad. "Not me! I'm not afraid of anything."

"I'm not afraid of anything either!" declared Alastair.

"Then why are you hiding out in history?" asked Tad.

Alastair shrugged and looked at the ground. I could tell she felt bad. "Well, we're not entirely ready for the burdens of office, that's all."

"Are you joking?" he said. "The White House is the greatest house in the world! Nanny, Nanko, and I get to play all we want because everybody else is too busy running the Civil War. Sometimes, if we're good, I get to sit on my pa's lap and hear what the Secretary of State has to say. My pa loves animals and the house is huge, so I get all the pets I want."

"My father's a great president too," declared Alastair. "Mark my words—he'll go down in history!"

There was a noise behind us, and the jalopy sputtered to life. Tad stared. The goats cowered behind him.

Alastair clapped her hands in delight. "Tipp, it started back up! Nice to meet you, Tad. No offense, but we're outta here!"

Scooping me up, she climbed inside. As she did, the

jalopy's voice kicked in, continuing our tour. ". . . built in 1874 but not fully utilized until . . ."

Tad shouted over it, "Nice to meet you, too! Hope you get to the right time. And you want some advice?"

The jalopy rose into the air. Alastair replied, "We'd love to hear it, but we're kind of pressed for time."

Cupping his hands around his mouth, Tad yelled to Alastair, "The White House is a once-in-a-lifetime chance. You'll be fine there, as long as you've got friends!"

Then, turning to the goats, Tad declared, "Okay, boys, saddle up. There's a war going on!"

He waved to us, then jumped into the chair. The goats took off, pulling him across the yard. The last we heard, the three of them were singing "The Battle Hymn of the Republic."

Meanwhile the jalopy continued to rise. Sitting back, Alastair grew thoughtful. "Just think, Tipp. Dad has all of history before him. He could become a president who's as great as Abraham Lincoln!"

"Oh, yeah," I muttered, "everything's great until you-know-who gets sent to the pound."

She set her chin firmly. "That won't happen. And

anyway, at least this contraption is running again, right? Next stop, my clubhouse and home, sweet home!"

Just then, the jalopy lurched and dove downward. There was a jolt, and suddenly we were back on the ground.

Alastair pounded the dashboard. "Are you kidding me?"

"Why did it stop?" I asked. "What's wrong?"

"Budget cuts. Gotta be." She glanced around the jalopy. "We need something to do while we're waiting for this crazy thing to make up its mind."

Something to do? Personally, I was planning a nervous breakdown.

Alastair set me down beside her, climbed into the backseat, and began rummaging around. "Look, here's the *Washington Post*! Okay, it's an old edition, but still . . ." She rummaged some more. "Hey, gummies! They'll keep your blood sugar up."

Just then, music started to play. This time it wasn't "The Battle Hymn of the Republic," unless they've added electric guitars.

I asked, "Where's that music coming from?"

"Beats me," said Alastair, thumbing through a stack

of newspapers. "Hey, this one's from 1968! You want to see the headlines?"

Just then, a voice called out from behind the bushes. "Turn that racket off!"

"Hippie music!" called another voice.

For a minute I thought the two goats were back. But these voices had a different accent—more of a Texas drawl.

The branches parted, and out trotted a pair of Beagles.

HE'S HIM

I don't have anything against Beagles. Of course, they're gross and obnoxious, and their ears hang down like fruit. Other than that, they're fine. But keep them away from me, okay? And whatever you do, don't let them talk!

"We hate hippie music!" said one Beagle.

"We like patriotic music!" said the other.

"American music!" said one.

"Texas music!" said the other.

Together they shouted, "So turn that racket off!"

See what I mean?

Alastair climbed out of the jalopy. "I'm sorry," she said, "but that isn't our music. It seems to be coming from the car."

The jalopy's voice kicked in again. "Welcome to President Lyndon Baines Johnson's moment in history! It all started in 1963 whennnnnnn . . ."

The voice slowed to a halt, and so did the music.

The first Beagle grinned. "That's better! Dad gum hippie music! It'll knock the sense clean outta your brain!"

"You're from the sixties?" asked Alastair.

"Darn tootin'!" answered the second Beagle. "Aren't you?"

"No!"

The second Beagle spotted me in the front seat. When I hopped down to meet him, he offered me his paw. "Shake, pardner!"

"Uh, gee . . ." I began.

"What's wrong?" he demanded.

I said, "It's just that . . . well, most dogs I know just sniff your butt."

"Aw, go ahead and shake," said the first Beagle. "He won't bite—at least, not until he knows you."

I shook the Beagle's paw.

"Who are you?" I asked his friend.

"He's Him," said the first Beagle.

"And she's Her," said the second.

"We're famous!" they shouted together. They threw back their heads and howled.

"I don't mean to be rude," said Alastair, "but we've never heard of you."

"'Course not!" said Her. "You're not from the sixties."

"We got our picture in *Life* magazine and started a great big controversy!" said Him. "You know, arguments and such."

"I'm mighty proud of it," said Her. "Controversy is what the sixties are all about. And we sure stirred some up."

Alastair introduced us, and Him's ears perked up. "Alastair and Tipp?" he asked. "Hey, aren't you those two we heard about that ran away from the White House?"

I glanced at Alastair. "Word sure spreads fast around here."

She told the Beagles, "All we're looking for is a nice, quiet place where we'll be safe. Controversy is the last thing we want."

"Well, you gotta be prepared for it," said Him.

Sticking his nose in my face, he shouted, "Are you *pre-pared*, boy?"

I jumped back. "N–no!" I stammered. "No, I'm not!"

Alastair picked me up and hugged me. "Leave Tipp alone! He's a little skittish."

"Belly full of jelly, huh?" said Her. "Can't have that if you're a White House pet."

"But I can't help it," I whined. "What was the controversy you started? Tell me so I can avoid it!"

"'Tweren't us that started it," said Her. "'Twas him."

I glanced at the other Beagle. "You mean, Him?"

"No, *him*! President Lyndon Baines Johnson, thirty-sixth president of the U. S. of A."

"Don't mess with Texas!" said Him.

They howled again.

I said, "This President Johnson—what did he do?"

"He picked us up by the ears," answered Him. "Paws clean off the ground."

I winced. "Didn't that hurt?"

"Heck no, we loved it!" said Her. "But the American public got hold of it, raised a stink, and the president's approval ratings shot through the floor. All because of a little ear-pulling, you believe that?"

Him snorted. "We didn't care. We knew our president was doing good: civil rights laws, health care for the poor and elderly, the Great Society, the War on Poverty . . ."

"Plus the war in Vietnam," said Alastair.

Suddenly there was silence. The Beagles glared at her.

"It's true," said Alastair. "I saw in my history book that President Johnson started the U.S. ground war in Vietnam . . ."

Him and Her started to growl.

Alastair continued, ". . . and he sent more troops to Vietnam. Made it hard for America to get out."

"You got a point?" snapped Her.

Alastair shrugged. "Not really. I was just—"

"We're proud of our president," Him declared. "You gotta stay tough in this game. Develop a thick hide."

"And real strong ears," said Her.

They howled again. Luckily, at that moment, the jalopy roared back to life.

"Sorry, gotta go," I told them.

"Fire hydrant's around back," said Him.

I hopped out of Alastair's arms and into the front

seat. "Actually, I meant that we have to leave. It's been great—well, mostly."

Climbing in beside me, Alastair asked the Beagles, "Do you have any parting advice?"

"Heck, yeah!" said Him. "Keep your friends close . . . and your enemies closer!"

"What kind of advice is that?" asked Alastair.

"Okay, then, how about this?" said Her. "Don't do anything fun when the cameras are rolling!"

They trotted off into the bushes, howling as they went. I held my ears. Thank goodness it was me holding my ears and not President Johnson!

BIRD POOP

The jalopy lurched forward, then sputtered and stopped.

Alastair groaned. "This is the worst piece of junk. We'll never get to my clubhouse!"

She kicked the tire as she climbed out. Harpsichord music started.

"I hate that music," I said. "Try kicking the tire again."

She did. The music stopped, and a mockingbird came fluttering down from the trees. I have nothing against birds, but this one looked a little rough, like a cross between a feather duster and an old pair of socks.

We ducked as he flew past us and watched him land on the door, where he squawked, "State your business."

Alastair ventured, "You mean, like, White House business?"

"What other kind of business is there? *Bwauk!*"

"We don't have any business with the White House," said Alastair. "In fact, we're trying to get away from it."

"*Bwauk!* State your business."

Alastair rolled her eyes. "Fine, whatever. I'm Alastair, and this is my dog Tipp."

The bird said, "If that's the tip, how bad was the service? *Bwauk!*"

"Yeah, good one," I muttered. "Never heard that one before."

Alastair said, "Okay, let's start at the beginning. I can see that you're a bird."

"I can see that you're a bird," he repeated.

"I'm not a bird!" she said.

"I'm not a bird!" he said.

"Will you stop copying me?" said Alastair.

"Sorry, it's an old habit," he said. "I'm Dick, the White House mockingbird, under the administration of Thomas Jefferson. I'm the president's favorite pet! Eat food right from his mouth. I do, I do, I do. *Tweep!*"

"From his mouth?" I said. "Yuck."

Dick squawked, "Word has it that you two are the new ones, right? You've been given a great opportunity!"

"Oh, really?" said Alastair. "An opportunity to what?"

"Affect public policy! Sculpt a nation!" He whipped out a map and unrolled it on the front seat. "I was there when President Jefferson approved this. It's the Louisiana Purchase! Doubled the size of our country!"

"So?" said Alastair. "That was in, like, 1800."

"It was 1803, Miss Smarty-Pants. But here's the important thing. If you look real close, you can see it."

I studied the map. "See what? Arkansas?"

"No!" exclaimed Dick. "You can see poop! Bird poop! *My* poop! Right there on the Louisiana Purchase."

"Ew," said Alastair.

Dick ruffled his feathers proudly. "I made my mark on history. I did, I did, I did. *Tweep!* President Jefferson let me fly around the Oval Office, at complete liberty. I made my mark on James Madison, Alexander Hamilton, and Aaron Burr. Okay, I'll admit it, that last time I was aiming. I made my mark all over history. If a bird can do it, so can you!"

Alastair said, "Thanks for the advice, but, in our time, a president can't exactly have a bird flying around the Oval Office."

"Even having a Chihuahua is a stretch," I added.

"Well, say what you want," said Dick, "but in my day we appreciated opportunity. We did our duty. So should you."

The jalopy shuddered back to life. Dick, surprised

by the sudden noise, fluttered into the air.

"*Bwauk!* This thing isn't safe!"

Alastair shook her head. "You can say that again."

"*Bwauk!* This thing isn't safe!"

Hastily rolling up his map, Dick took off toward the trees. As he disappeared among the branches, he called back to us, "Don't run away from opportunity. And stay close to your friends. *Tweep!*"

I watched him go, then inspected the door where he'd been sitting.

"Well, he was right about one thing," I said.

"What's that?" asked Alastair.

"He left his mark on history."

9

BARELY AN APPETIZER

Something was making me nervous. Okay, everything was making me nervous. But there was one thing in particular.

Dick the mockingbird had left. The jalopy had sputtered to a stop—again. Alastair had opened the hood to see if she could restart the engine, leaving me alone on the front seat.

That's when it happened. I got a creepy, tingly sensation on the back of my neck.

"Do you ever have the feeling you're being watched?" I asked Alastair.

"Don't be silly," she called from under the hood. "There's no one for miles."

"I'm not so sure," I said. Lifting my nose into the air, I sniffed. "My keen, quivering doggie nose smells something . . ."

I did a quick scan of the area and saw nothing but an alligator.

An alligator!

I tried to tell Alastair. "Alli-Alli-Al—"

"Tipp-Tipp-Tipp—See how annoying it is when you do that?"

"A-A-A-A-A-A—"

She said, "Alastair! Call me Alastair! You know how I hate nicknames."

"G-G-G-G-G-G—"

"What? Will you speak up?"

"ALLIGATOR!" I finally screamed.

I hopped from the car and raced around to the front, where I did a flying leap into Alastair's arms. By that time, she had looked out from under the hood and was staring in shock.

The alligator was big and long and ugly—basically, a pair of jaws with legs. He lunged toward us, his teeth snapping. We dove to the side, barely avoiding him.

He grinned. I shivered. This guy had cavities bigger than I was.

"Ah, *mes chers*," he oozed, "almost got you, did I not?"

"What the heck?" said Alastair. "An alligator with a French accent?"

"But of course," he said, starting toward us again. "Now, come to papa."

Papa? I had news for him. My father was twelve inches long, not twelve feet. And his teeth were sharp, but there were only three of them.

Alastair, meanwhile, didn't believe her eyes. "Oh, come on! When did an alligator ever live in the White House? This never happened, and I'll prove it."

The alligator closed in on us. Meanwhile, Alastair hurried back to the front seat, set me down, and began thumbing through her history book. Now, history's great. I love it. But there are some things that are more important. Like staying alive, for instance.

I said, "Uh, Alastair . . ."

The alligator licked his chops and murmured, "Ah, *cherie*, there is much about the White House that no one ever wrote down. Lots of history that nobody talks about. . . . Lots of history that maybe isn't so true . . . but it makes a rollicking good story, *oui*?"

She flipped through the pages. "But there was no alligator in the White House, ever. Unless it was stuffed."

The alligator grinned and opened his jaws wide. His mouth was like the Grand Canyon with a tongue.

"He's not stuffed!" I croaked.

"Don't worry, Tipp," Alastair assured me. "This is totally a myth."

"That's a lot of teeth for a myth!" I said.

He gazed at me, the way you might look at a hot fudge sundae. "Now, if you please," he purred, "just one little taste, *s'il vous plaît*?"

I could smell his breath. It was strong enough to peel the paint off Air Force One.

"Alastair, save me!" I squeaked. "I'm too young to die!"

Finally she looked up. Slamming the book shut, she turned to the alligator. "Now, see here, you . . . you White House alligator pet–type animal! We didn't come all this way to end up as somebody's meal!"

The alligator laughed. "But, *cherie*, this little creature is barely an appetizer!"

Just then we heard a noise in the bushes, and a man came charging out. He had a powdered wig, wore a fancy uniform, and carried a big leash.

"*Sacre bleu!*" the man told the alligator. "Finally I find you! Did I not tell you once, did I not tell you twice, did I not tell you three times. . . . There is no eating the White House guests!"

The alligator sighed. "I was only having a little fun."

"I warn you now," the man told him. "Back away from the pigeon."

"He's a Chihuahua!" said Alastair.

The alligator backed away, and I jumped into Alastair's arms. She eyed the man. "Who are you, anyway?"

He smiled and bowed low. "Marie-Joseph Paul Yves Roch Gilbert du Motier, Marquis de Lafayette, at your service, *mademoiselle!*"

"That's a mouthful!" said Alastair.

"Not even close," sighed the alligator.

"And you?" Lafayette asked her. "With whom do I have the pleasure of speaking?"

She blushed. "Alastair Lodge. I guess you could say I'm the new First Daughter. My father was just elected president."

"Ah, congratulations, *mademoiselle*." Lafayette shook his finger at the alligator. "And as for you, *monsieur*, if you continue this behavior, you will go back to the Louisiana bayou where you came from."

"But General Lafayette," whined the alligator, "you promised I could see Paris! The Seine! Le Cathédrale Notre Dame!"

"Very well," said Lafayette. "But only if you don't go nibbling up American children. They are our allies and friends."

Alastair checked her book again. "So, General Lafayette, if we're friends, then maybe you can answer a question for me. I see here that you sided with us in the American Revolution, then went on to fight in the French Revolution. There are streets, buildings, towns, and schools named after you."

"Ah, *cherie*," he said, "you make me blush."

"But," she went on, "I can't find any sign of the alligator. Where did he come from?"

Lafayette chuckled. "My apologies, little First Daughter of les États-Unis! The alligator, he was a gift to President John Quincy Adams. But President Adams, he was terribly . . . how you say, uncomfortable with the presence of a reptile in the East Room. So the alligator came to me."

Leaning over, he looped the leash around the alligator's neck. "And now, I regret to say, we must be leaving. Paris is waiting!"

He gave a low bow, and they headed for the trees. The alligator called, "Good-bye, *cherie*! Good-bye, my little appetizer!"

Lafayette yanked the leash. "One more word and I will make fancy boots out of you!"

He turned back to us and waved. "*Au revoir*, little First Daughter! Have a wonderful four years!"

HOLY COW!

Alastair flopped down on the front seat, and I climbed into her lap. I could tell she was discouraged, and, with Alastair, that's pretty unusual.

"What if we never get to my clubhouse?" she said.

I nodded. "What if we never get back at all?"

The jalopy must have heard us because the engine clattered to life. Then, just as quickly, it died.

"Make up your mind!" I shrieked.

"Hey, are you okay?" asked Alastair.

"No! I'm a nervous wreck!"

"But at least we're together," she said. "Right?"

Before I could say anything, the bushes parted and a cow flounced out. She was a walking solution to the famous riddle, "What's black and white and red all over?" Answer: An angry cow.

"I did not do it!" she said.

I stared at her, amazed at how many animals we had met. "Holy cow!"

"Cow?" she snapped. "I'll have you know that I am not just a cow. I'm Pauline Wayne, and I'm a Holstein-Friesian!"

"Oh, sorry," I said.

She shook her head. "Disgraceful manners for a mouse."

"He's a Chihuahua!" said Alastair.

Pauline hardly noticed. She just kept rattling on. "I tell you, I didn't do it. The very thought—I am a lady!"

Alastair stepped out of the jalopy, and I followed.

"I don't understand," said Alastair. "What did you do?"

"Nothing!" answered Pauline. "I have stated repeatedly that I did *not* do it."

We were getting nowhere fast. I turned to Alastair. "A cow at the White House? What kind of president would do that?"

Pauline drew herself up to her full height, which

was about twenty-five of me. "President William H. Taft, that's who! He's a true gentleman. He has respect for a lady. Not like those reporters."

"Reporters?" said Alastair. "What did they do?"

"You wouldn't believe it if I told you. But of course, nice girls don't talk about such things."

Maybe nice girls didn't, but it was obvious she did. Unable to hold back, Pauline exclaimed, "Really, it's appalling that public morals have deteriorated to such a degree that my flawless work ethic and sterling repu- tation would be called into question!" With that, she burst into tears.

Alastair hurried to her side. "Hey, hey, hey. It can't be that bad. . . . Can it?"

"Oh, you don't know," blubbered Pauline. "You haven't lived in the public eye as I have."

"Well, I'm about to," said Alastair. "And so is my dog. We can sympathize."

Pauline wiped her eyes. "Such a scandal . . . in the papers . . ."

"What did the papers say?" asked Alastair.

"Well, there was a man. From Ohio. And he claimed . . ." She glanced at us, embarrassed.

This was getting old. "Come on, lady," I said, "spit it out."

"He claimed that he *milked* me! On the *South Lawn*! Those vile reporters picked up the story. It was quickly disproven, of course. But the damage to my delicate nature was already done. Oh, to live under a cloud of scandal . . ."

Alastair said, "Was President Taft mad at you?"

"Of course not!" answered Pauline. "Upstanding gentleman that he was, he whisked me away to live in Wisconsin, where there was less public scrutiny."

Alastair exclaimed, "That's exactly what we're trying to do! We need to get away from those people in the White House. They want to take my dog away from me."

"Oh you mustn't let them do such a thing, my dears!" said Pauline.

"That's why we're running away," Alastair explained. "But now the whole thing has backfired and we can't get back."

"Learn from my shocking story," said Pauline. "Don't let those horrid reporters demean your reputation."

I said, "Actually, it's a guy named Miles."

She didn't hear me. She had already turned and was making her way back to the bushes. "The humiliation!" she cried. "Oh, the humiliation!"

If you ask me, the man from Ohio had nothing on her. Pauline was milking her story for all it was worth.

11

ARE YOU A SPY?

Suddenly, the jalopy sputtered to life. We raced over and jumped in. As we did, the voice cranked up again.

"Back in 1870, following the dark days of the Civil Warrrrrrrrrr . . ."

It clattered to a stop.

"Great. Just great," sobbed Alastair. "We're stuck here, Tipp, stuck traveling through time. We'll never get home!"

"Alastair, don't cry," I begged. "I'm here for you. Nothing could ever, ever make me forget you."

"Pssst!" someone said.

I took one look at where the voice came from and forgot all about Alastair.

A dog stood there . . . but not just any dog. She was white and gray, with fur you could get lost in. Her eyes sparkled, and her tail wagged. Her ears flipped a little at the top. So did my heart.

I tried to say something, but all that came out was a squeak.

She spoke with a Russian accent. Her voice was low and sultry. "You ask who I am? I tell you who I am. I am . . . Pushinka."

"P-p-p-pushinka!" I stuttered. "That's a beautiful name."

She smiled. "Translation: Fluffy."

"You certainly are," I replied.

Eyes trained on me, she circled and gave me a wink. "You are some cute little guy. Anyone ever tell you that?"

"Never," I said.

Alastair cleared her throat.

"Well, actually, one person did," I admitted. "This is Alastair."

Pushinka barely noticed her. "So, tell me cute, little guy. What is it you want to be when you grow up?"

Drawing myself up to my full height of ten

inches—okay, six inches—I declared, "I *am* grown up."

"Well then, take a look at this," answered Pushinka, stroking her fur. "You like my coat? My delicate paws? My swishy tail?"

I gulped. "Do I have to pick one?"

"Oh, for Pete's sake!" exclaimed Alastair.

Pushinka looked up at her, wounded. "I cannot help it if I devastate men. I am Russian, after all. And you know what they say: All is fair in love and war. Especially the Cold War."

"Cold War?" I said. "Are you a spy?"

"Hah!" scowled Pushinka. "You American dogs are all alike. You think that with one look at your beautiful manliness I will spill my classified Russian secret!"

"Secret?" said Alastair.

Pushinka leaned in close. I sniffed her perfume: Essence of Kibble. "Ah, I know a secret that would curl your tail! My mother was Strelka. You know Strelka?"

"Not really," I said.

"She was the first Russian dog put into outer space! Before people went there, they sent dogs. Ah, yes, Pushinka has a secret."

Alastair shrugged. Somehow, she wasn't as impressed

as I was. "Okay, Fluffy, we'll bite. What's your big secret?"

Smiling proudly, Pushinka strutted back and forth in front of us. "You want to know my big, scary Russian secret as we teeter on the brink of nuclear disaster? My secret that could end the world, as two superpowers stare each other down from across a frightened globe?"

"Yes!" I said. "Out with it!"

"My big secret is . . ."

I braced myself. Alastair yawned.

"My secret is that I have no secret!"

"Huh?" I said.

Pushinka sighed. When she spoke again, her accent was gone. She sounded like any other mutt on the block.

"A real letdown, right?" she asked. "How do you think I feel? The Russian premier, Nikita Khrushchev, brought me over as a gift for First Lady Jacqueline Kennedy. The Americans took one look at me and thought, *She must be a KGB spy with a little doggie transmitter that sends top secret signals to one of those newfangled Soviet satellites.* But no, not me. The big, glamorous Soviet spy dog is just a dog."

"Don't say that!" I told her. "You're special!"

"Sorry, cutie. I got married off to one of the White House boys—a terrier named Charlie. You know how they are. We had a couple of pupniks and now I'm an ordinary housewife."

I still couldn't believe it. "But you could never be ordinary!"

She shook her head sadly. "From the corridors of power at the Kremlin and the White House . . . to Wednesday nights at the club playing Mahjong with the girls . . . to Saturday nights at home with Charlie watching Ed Sullivan. What a comedown."

As she finished, the jalopy sprang to life again.

"Well, it's been nice knowing you," Alastair told Pushinka, "but I'm afraid we have to go. Come on, Tipp."

I couldn't bear the thought. As Alastair stepped into the jalopy, I cried out, "Pushinka, I've never met anyone like you before in my life!"

"I know, baby."

"I don't want to leave you!" I said.

"They never do."

Alastair said, "Time to go, Tipp."

I begged Pushinka, "Come with me!"

She gazed at me with those deep brown eyes. "Oh, my nervous little darling, the Cold War is over. You have new work—being a White House pet. It's the most important work a dog can do!"

The jalopy started to rise.

"Tipp, hurry!" said Alastair.

I said, "Pushinka, I can't face the future without you!"

"Yes, you can," she said. "You will, because you are strong! You are brave! You are pure! You are . . . First Chihuahua!"

"Now!" yelled Alastair. She leaned out of the jalopy, and I hopped into her arms.

Pushinka lifted her paw in farewell. "Good luck, kids." She waved as we rose into the air.

First Chihauhua? Hey, I liked the sound of that.

MY PERSONAL HERO

The jalopy rose, then started to buck and shimmy in midair.

"What's happening?" I whimpered.

"Maybe you could tell me," snapped Alastair. "After all, you're First Chihuahua."

I said, "You're not mad, are you?"

"What do you think? You were going to leave me stranded alone in history for a fake accent and some big brown eyes? Don't ever do that to me again."

Just then, the jalopy dropped like a rock. Alastair held me close, and I shut my eyes. When I opened them again, the jalopy was indoors and music was playing.

"Welcome to the East Room!" announced the jalopy.

I said, "We must be back in the White House. How did that happen?"

"I'm not sure," said Alastair. "But I do recognize that tune: 'Brother, Can You Spare a Dime?'. I had an uncle who used to play it on the piano. It's from the 1930s. You know, the Great Depression."

"What's the East Room?" I asked Alastair.

"It's where they have receptions and parties for dignitaries and heads of state."

I looked around. There were high ceilings and fancy chandeliers. There were also three dogs. But they weren't just any dogs.

"Alastair, look!" I exclaimed. "It's Fala! And Laddie Boy and Millie!"

"Fala and . . . who?" she asked.

"Are you kidding? These are the most popular presidential dogs in history. Oh, Alastair, if they can't tell us how to get back, then no one can."

Fala approached the jalopy. He was a Scottish Terrier with a proud tilt to his head. I started to quiver. It was one of the greatest moments of my life.

Seeing me, Fala smiled. With a thick Scottish brogue, he said, "No need to be nervous, lad. We put on our collars the same way you do."

"Please, sir," I told him, "allow me the honor." Hopping out of the jalopy, I sniffed each dog.

Alastair said, "You know, Tipp, maybe just a hand-shake . . ."

When I finished, I turned to introduce my new friends.

"Alastair, this Airedale Terrier is Laddie Boy, the favorite pet of President Warren G. Harding. He presided over the Easter Egg Roll of 1923 on the White House lawn and advocated the first eight-hour work-day for watchdogs."

Laddie Boy gave a loud bark. "Gotta speak for the masses, you know."

"There was a newspaper article written about him every single day!" I said.

Laddie Boy added, "And no one photographs as beautifully as an Airedale, that's for sure."

"In fact," I said, "everybody was so busy watching Laddie Boy that they almost missed Teapot Dome. That was a big scandal during the Harding administration."

There was an awkward silence. Fala snickered, and Laddie Boy glared at him. "Shut up, Fala."

I quickly jumped in. "And this English Springer Spaniel is Millie, favorite of the first President Bush. She wrote a book about the White House that raised almost nine hundred thousand dollars for charity. And that was after having six kids!"

"Oh," said Millie, "I was really just like any other single, working mother . . ."

"I loved your book!" I exclaimed. "I read it, like, eighty times."

"I'll make sure you get an autographed copy, dear," she told me.

I turned back to Alastair. "And this magnificent Scottish Terrier . . . this is Fala."

Fala shuffled his paws, embarrassed. "Aw, now . . ."

"Fala never left President Franklin D. Roosevelt's side," I told her. "Fala was with Roosevelt when he met Churchill and they changed the course of World War II! There's a statue of him at Roosevelt's memorial. Plus, he was a private in the War Dog Fund Drive—he even gave up his rubber bone for the war effort."

"A sacrifice, for sure," said Fala. "But it was good old American determination that showed those Nazis what was what!"

"You're my personal hero," I told him. "There are so many questions I want to ask you. . . ."

"Ask away, my little friend."

I said, "What was it like that time they left you behind and President Roosevelt had to send a Navy ship to find you?"

"I won't lie to you, lad. That did not happen."

"What? He didn't send a destroyer to bring you home?"

Fala shook his head. "Sorry, wee one. It's a good story, for sure, but I'm honor bound to set you straight. Legends are fine, but when it comes right down to it, I'm only canine."

I said, "Imagine that, Alastair. A dog, just like me!"

Fala said, "Now, don't get me wrong, lad. Being the First Pet makes you a witness to history. I was there with my president from the Depression through World War II. I was with him when he met Stalin at the Yalta Conference. I went to Quebec for a secret meeting with Winston Churchill. I was even with him at his death bed at Warm Springs, Georgia."

"Wow." I breathed.

Meanwhile, Alastair stepped out of the jalopy and approached. "It's nice to meet you all, really. But Tipp and I are lost, and I don't mind telling you that I'm worried. Is there any way you can help us?"

"Help you?" said Fala. "Why, lass, we'd be happy to. Helping is what we do best!"

I AM MAGNIFICENT

Laddie Boy said, "Helping is what we're all about. We're man's best friend."

"*President's* best friend," said Fala.

Millie suggested, "Just ask us your question, and we'll try to answer it fairly, honestly, and accurately."

"Because we know a lot," said Fala. "We've seen a lot. And we are here to serve."

They gazed at us, waiting eagerly. I was proud to be in the same room with them.

"Well," said Alastair, "it all started because I was afraid Tipp was going to be taken away from me. We wanted to go back in time to a safer place. Of course, now we see that it was a dumb idea to run away from the White House."

Fala stared at us. "You left the White House?"

"Voluntarily?" asked Millie. "You weren't kidnapped?"

Laddie Boy said, "You left the greatest job in the world? You left the greatest *house* in the world?"

Alastair tried to explain. "We just wanted to escape. . . ."

Fala shook his head sadly. "Well, this changes everything."

"What do you mean?" I asked.

He glanced at the others. "Tell them."

Millie said, "Laddie Boy never ran away from anything in his life!"

Laddie Boy said, "Millie Bush made a name for herself! And Fala . . . well, Fala . . ."

Fala puffed out his chest. "I'm not a clue in all those crossword puzzles because I shirked *my* duty."

"Now wait a minute," said Alastair. "We didn't shirk our duty."

"Lass, you ran away from the White House," said Fala.

Laddie Boy said, "We never ran away. I sat in my

very own cabinet chair every single day in office. Don't you think I would rather have played fetch?"

Millie added, "Do you know the sacrifices I made raising six puppies and pursuing a full-time writing career?"

Fala nodded. "What kind of pet leaves when the going gets . . . well, *ruff*!"

I looked at Alastair. Tears welled up in her eyes. She said, "Please! Please! You're the most powerful White House pets ever. You've got to help us."

"Well," said Laddie Boy, "we certainly are the most powerful White House pets ever. That's true."

Fala added, "But we can't be seen helping people who would run away from their duty."

"So, that's it?" asked Alastair. "You're not going to help?"

"Sorry, lass," said Fala.

Alastair picked me up and gave me a hug. "Come on, Tipp. There are no answers here."

Fala and the others turned to go. Watching them, I felt something rise up inside of me. It might have been my breakfast. Then again, maybe it was something else. Instead of quivering or shaking or running away, I was getting mad! It was a brand-new feeling. I'm not sure where it came from, but it got bigger and bigger, until finally I couldn't hold it inside any longer.

"No!" I yelled at them. "Bad dogs!"

Fala cocked his head. "Beg your pardon?"

"You heard me," I said. "Bad dogs! The Fala I read about would never have refused a dog in need. And now you're saying you won't help us because it's bad for your *image*? Well, that's just fine! We don't need you or your help, and you know why?"

"No," said Fala. "Why?"

"Because she's the First Daughter, Alastair Lodge, and nothing gets her down, not for long. And I—well, the history books may not know about me yet, but they will. You wait and see. I'll make history because I am . . . First Chihuahua!"

Alastair said, "Tipp, are you okay?"

"I'm not just okay," I told her. "I am magnificent!"

I thrust my chest out. When I spoke to the other dogs, suddenly I had a Spanish accent that would have made Zorro proud. "I will bite your ears if you defy me! I will nibble your nails if you dis me! I will rip the soles from your heels! I am First Chihuahua. *Yo soy El Primer Chihuahua!*"

Turning to Alastair, I said, "Come on, let's get out of here."

Laddie Boy stared at me in amazement. "Did you see that, Fala? If I didn't know better, I'd say that he was . . ."

"What?" asked Fala.

"Presidential!" said Laddie Boy.

RUNNING DOESN'T WORK

Alastair watched the three dogs leave, then gave me a big hug. For once, I didn't feel like a rabbit or a mouse. I was a Chihuahua—First Chihuahua!

"That was amazing!" she said. "You kicked some serious famous doggie butt!"

I felt ten feet tall. Well, maybe three and a half feet. But for me, that's big!

Alastair set me down on the floor. "Strut it, Tipp! Work it. You are one mean dog."

My leg shot out. I swiveled a hip. My head bobbed, and my paws jabbed. Hey, I had moves! I didn't know I had moves.

I was just getting started when the room suddenly

got darker, and there was a hissing sound.

"Did you hear that?" asked Alastair.

Suddenly I didn't feel quite so brave. Shivering, I said, "I have a bad feeling about this."

Alastair looked at me. Her eyes were as big as dinner bowls. "Max warned us about this. If there's hissing, then there must be . . ."

"A snake!" we yelled together.

I jumped back into her arms. "I'm sorry, Alastair. It was my fault. I hit the red button."

"That's okay," she said. "Just remember what Max told us: 'Don't talk to the snake.'"

We looked around, waiting. We were alone in the room.

"S-s-so," said a voice. "The time has-s-s come!"

Alastair whimpered, "I want to go home. I want my mom!"

"It's s-s-so good to have visitors," said the voice. "I never get to s-s-see anyone down here."

The old Tipp would have panicked. He would have quivered, wailed, and maybe even thrown up on the carpet. But I was the new Tipp. I was First Chihuahua. And it was time to act.

Leaping from Alastair's arms, I spread my paws and stood up straight. "Okay, who's talking? Show yourself!"

Out of the shadows slithered a big green snake. Okay, it was scary, but I decided to look at the bright side: Even though the snake was long, it wasn't any taller than I was.

The snake circled around us, getting closer with each turn. Alastair cowered behind me. If there's anything in the world that scares her, it's snakes.

"Please, Tipp," she pleaded, "let's get out of here."

I shook my head. "No, we're not going to run again. Running doesn't work."

The snake grinned. "S-s-so happy to hear that. I get lonely down here. S-s-so lonely."

Slithering around our ankles, the snake hissed, "My name is-s-s-s Emily Spinach. I heard that you ran away from the White House, and you've been busy asking questions. Do you have any questions you'd like to as-s-s-sk me?"

Alastair stuttered, "W-w-well, actually, we were told . . . I m-m-mean, it was suggested that we . . ."

"Yes-s-s?"

"That we not talk to the snake!" Alastair blurted,

cringing. "So please, just leave us alone!"

I felt a deadly calm settle over me. Alastair was scared. She needed my help. And I, the First Chihuahua, would come to her rescue.

"Let me handle this," I told her.

Stepping forward, I said to Emily, "Look, lady, you're making my friend uncomfortable, so you'd better just back off!"

She hesitated. "I mean no offens-s-s-se."

I felt more courage with every word. "And you better not try anything, 'cause I am one mean, vicious dog when it comes to protecting my First Daughter. I am scary! I am crazy! I am . . ."

Suddenly the Spanish accent came back. I felt like eating a taco or something.

"I am chewer of slippers!" I said. "I am biter of kneecaps! If you lay one hand on this girl, you will be sorry! Every night you will drool the drool of remorse on the pillow of regret!"

Pretty good, huh? Where do I get this stuff?

My leg wiggled, and my head started to bob. I started dancing around, showing a few moves. "I am bad, lady! Oh, yeah. If you touch the First Daughter,

I will seek you out! I will hunt you down. I will run circles around you until you surrender! There will be no mercy from *El Primer Chihuahua!*"

I gave her all my best material, which is why I was surprised at her reaction.

She laughed.

I stared at her. "You dare to laugh at *El Primer Chihuahua?* Seriously, it worked before."

Emily shook her head. "No, no, I'm not laughing at you. I'm laughing because . . . well, the truth is, I'm harmless."

Alastair said, "Harmless? But you're a snake."

"I'm a garter snake," Emily explained. "Do you really think we eat children? I don't even like to hiss. I just do it for special occasions."

"So, you're not poisonous?" said Alastair.

"Of course not. There are no poisonous snakes in the White House. There are skunks, spiders, and pigs—and I'm not just talking about the animals."

I had been angry. Now I was curious. "Do you live in the White House?"

Emily slithered closer and coiled up at Alastair's feet. "I belong to President Theodore Roosevelt's daughter,

Alice. But no one likes me, not even the president. 'Alice Roosevelt,' he says, 'it's unseemly for the First Daughter to be cavorting with a snake! Why can't you have a girlish pet? A kitten, a bunny, or a canary? That would be bully!'"

"How do you cope?" asked Alastair.

"Oh, sometimes it's difficult," said Emily. "Snakes are very sensitive, you know—sensitive to sound and vibration. But Alice is my friend, no matter what."

Alastair said, "Someone told us, 'Keep your friends close and your enemies closer.'"

"That's the silliest thing I've ever heard," snorted Emily. "Your friends are the ones who get you through difficult times, not your enemies."

Alastair sighed with relief. "That's the most sensible thing I've heard all day."

"Maybe so," I reminded her, "but none of it means anything if we can't get back."

Emily said, "Ah, so now you want to get back? I was told you were looking for a clubhouse."

Alastair glanced at me, and I gave her a nod. With a determined look on her face, she turned to Emily. "Not anymore. That clubhouse is in the past. I'd much rather live in the present. My dad is in the White House and he needs us by his side."

Alastair reached down and picked me up. "So," she told Emily, "what about it? Can you help us get home?"

"Home to the White House?" I asked.

"Home to the White House!" said Alastair.

Emily studied the jalopy. "Well, if your car's broken, I'm afraid I can't help you. But I know someone who can."

She gave a loud hiss. The doors to the East Room opened, and bright red roadster came puttering through. Behind the wheel was a young woman in an old-fashioned skirt.

Alastair stared at the driver. "Is it? Can it possibly be?"

She grabbed her history book and leafed through it. Finally she found what she was looking for.

"It is, it really is!" she exclaimed. "Tipp, look at this photo. That driver is Alice Roosevelt!"

TIME TO GO HOME

The car skidded to a stop and Alice Roosevelt jumped out.

"Emily, did you call?" she asked. "Whatever it is, be quick about it. I've got a peace treaty to broker, a senator to meet, and a party to throw!"

Emily said, "These are my new friends, Alastair and Tipp. They're trying to get back to their time, but their jalopy is broken. Can you help?"

Alice grinned. "Sure! Anything for Emily Spinach!" She went back to her roadster and began rummaging around inside.

Alastair ventured closer. "You really are Alice Roosevelt? You're the most famous First Daughter of all! They called you 'The Other Washington Monument!'"

Alice looked up. "Hah! Never was sure how I felt about being compared to a big block of stone."

A moment later, Alice found what she was looking for. It was a toolbox. Carrying it to the jalopy, she shook her head in amazement. "This old thing? I haven't thought about it in years. I didn't know they still allowed kids to play in it."

Alastair said, "You've seen it before?"

"Seen it? This jalopy and I got into more trouble than you could shake a stick at!"

"Stick?" I said. "Did someone say stick?"

"You talk!" exclaimed Alice, smiling at me. "I thought you might."

Emily rolled her eyes. "Don't get him started."

I bowed low. Okay, I was already low, but I bowed anyway. "I am honored to meet you, Miss Roosevelt. *Yo soy El Primer Chihuahua*, but you can call me First Chihuahua."

"I like your style," said Alice.

Taking a wrench from the toolbox, she lifted the hood of the jalopy and stuck her head inside. As she worked, Alastair opened the book again.

"I've read about some of the things you did," she told Alice. "Didn't you meet the Emperor of Japan?"

"Yeah, that was me."

Alastair checked another page. "Did you actually bury a voodoo doll of President Taft's wife on the White House lawn?"

"That made the history books?"

"It sure did," said Alastair. "And did you really wear a boa constrictor around your neck?"

"I'm embarrassed to admit that it's true," said Alice. She glanced up at Alastair. "When you get back to the White House, I hope you'll be better behaved than I was."

Alastair's eyes opened wide. "Did you say *when* I get back? Does this mean you'll be able to fix the jalopy?"

"Sure!" said Alice. "You just have to know which bolt to tighten, which gear to adjust . . ."

She reached back under the hood and gave the wrench a twist. The jalopy roared to life!

Alice closed the hood, put the wrench back in the toolbox, and brushed off her hands. "What did I tell you? Pointed straight for the White House."

"*My* White House? The one where my dad is?"

"Absolutely," said Alice.

Alastair threw her arms around Alice. "Oh, thank you! Thank you so much!"

Me? I felt some moves coming on. My hip jutted out and my leg kicked in the air.

Alice watched me. "Is he all right?"

"That's just Tipp," said Alastair. "What would I ever do without him?"

Closing her history book, Alastair picked me up and climbed back into the jalopy. "Come on, Tipp. It's time to go home."

Turning to Alice, she declared, "We won't forget you. We won't forget any of this."

"Have fun," said Alice. "Enjoy every minute!"

Alastair took hold of the steering wheel. "Thanks for your advice, Emily Spinach. Tipp and I will hang onto each other very tightly."

"Come back and visit us-s-s," said Emily.

Alice said, "When you think about it, we're not going anywhere. After all, we're history!"

We lifted off the ground and went zooming into the sky, back to the twenty-first century. As we flew through the clouds, I climbed into Alastair's lap.

"I'll be brave for you," I said.

"And I'll be strong for you," said Alastair.

I puffed out my chest. "After all . . . *yo soy El Primer Chihuahua!*"

A few minutes later the clouds parted, and the White House came into view, gleaming in the sunlight. Alastair smiled, but I could tell she was thinking.

"Tipp," she said, "do you think Max really meant for us to get lost? To learn from history?"

"I'm not sure. But as someone said, 'The more you know about the past, the better you are prepared for the future.'"

"Who said that?" Alastair asked. "Fala?"

I grinned. "It was Teddy Roosevelt. After all, you're not the only one who's been boning up on White House history!"

A few minutes later, we landed on the White House lawn. Max and Milo were waiting for us.

"Told you they'd show up," said Max.

From the expression on Milo's face, he was obviously as cranky as ever. "Where have you been? I've been looking all over for you!"

Alastair stepped out of the jalopy, with me in one arm and her history book in the other.

"Can't talk now," she said. "Too much to do! We have fan mail to answer, charities to address, books to write, autographs to sign, people to unite. We're going to be very busy!"

Hopping out of her arms, I gave Milo a couple of quick moves and shot him a mean glare.

"About that new dog," I told him. "You even think about getting one, and I will hunt you down like the crazed mongrel that I am! You will never get a moment's rest. I will chew on your toes! I will gnaw the laces from your shoes! I am biter of hemlines! I am chaser of squirrels! *Yo soy El Primer Chihuahua!*"

Milo gaped at me. "Did that dog just . . . talk?"

"A talking dog?" said Max. "What kind of crazy nonsense is that?"

"It's the pressure," said Milo, shaking his head. "It's got to be the pressure. I don't think I'm cut out for this job."

Max pulled a package from his pocket and offered it to Milo. "Would you like a lemon drop?"

"Hey, thanks," said Milo. He took one from the

package and put it into his mouth. I had a feeling Milo was going to be just fine.

"Come on, Tipp," said Alastair, smiling. "We've got work to do—together!"

She gave me a hug, and we headed for the White House.

I couldn't be sure, but as we walked off, I thought I heard Max say softly, "Thanks again, Emily Spinach."

Even more softly, far away but somehow very nearby, a voice answered, "Anytime, Max-x-x. Anytime."

MYSTERY. ADVENTURE. HOMEWORK.

ENTER THE WORLD OF DAN GUTMAN.